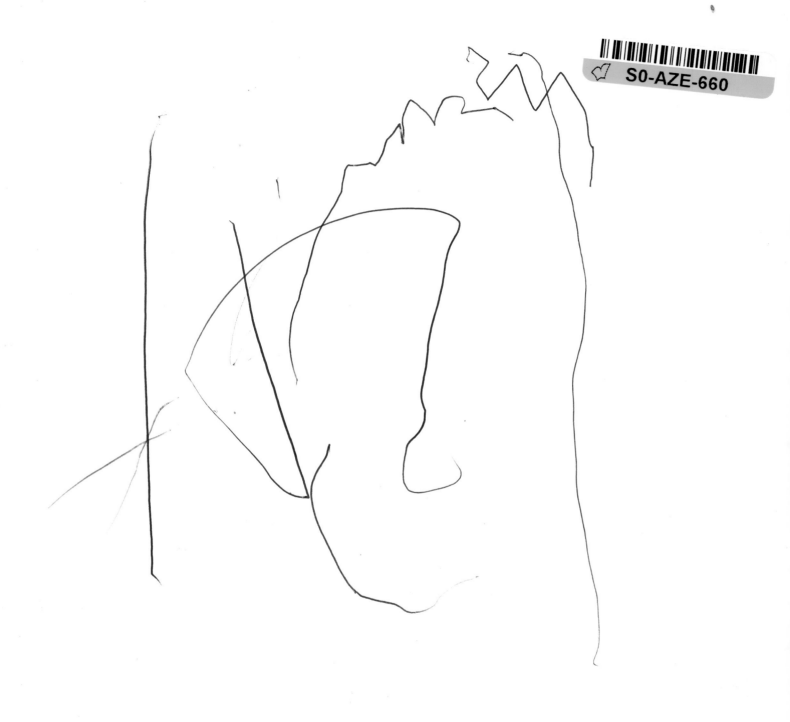

The Berenstain Bears®
The Wonderful Scents of Christmas
A SCRATCH AND SNIFF STORY

Mike Berenstain

Based on the characters created by
Stan and Jan Berenstain

The Berenstain Bears: The Wonderful Scents of Christmas
Copyright © 2022 by Berenstain Publishing, Inc.
All rights reserved. Manufactured in Malaysia.
No part of this book may be used or reproduced in any manner whatsoever without written permission
except in the case of brief quotations embodied in critical articles and reviews. For information address
HarperCollins Children's Books, a division of HarperCollins Publishers, 195 Broadway, New York, NY 10007.
www.harpercollinschildrens.com
ISBN 978-0-06-302439-7
Typography by Rick Farley
22 23 24 25 26 IMG 10 9 8 7 6 5 4 3 2 1 ❖ First Edition

The Bear family is trudging through the snowy woods to pick out a perfect Christmas tree.

"Here's a nice one!" says Sister.

"Yes!" agrees Brother. "Not too small, not too tall."

"Not too bushy!" adds Mama.

"Not too skimpy!" says Papa.

"Yay!" shouts Honey.

Papa chops down the perfect tree. There is a wonderful *pine tree smell!*

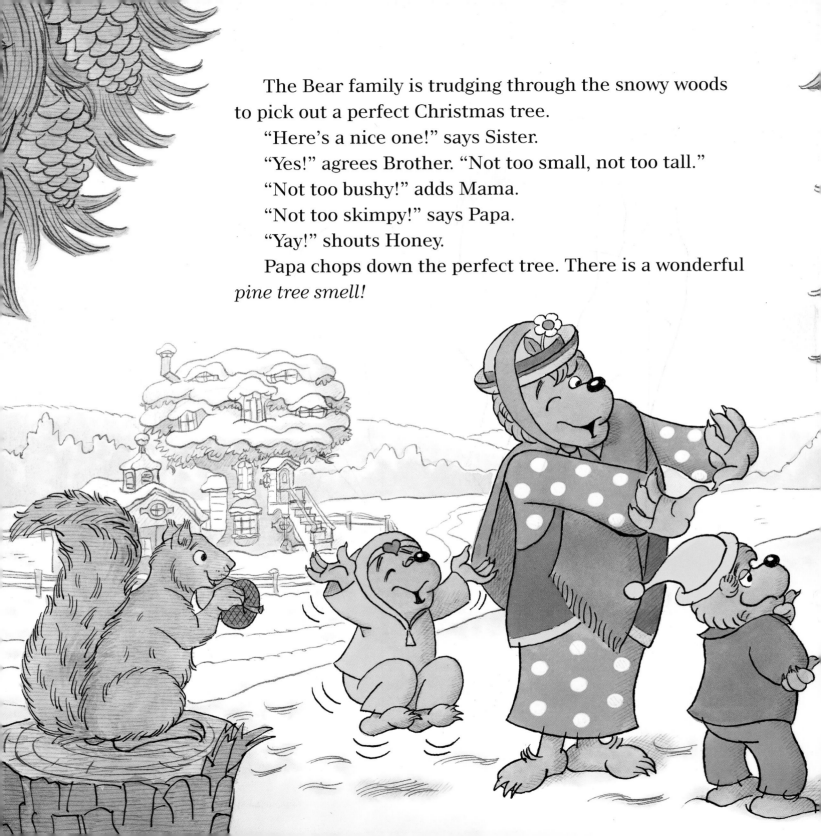

Back home, they pause to finish putting up
holly wreaths on their windows and doors.
Holly has a deep, rich green color with bright red
berries. Birds love those holly berries.

"Hello there, neighbor!" says Mama to a
bold bird swooping down to gobble some berries.
"Merry Christmas!"

The bears bundle into their home with their freshly cut tree. They're still cold from their snowy outing, so they all gather around the fireplace to get warm. They rub their hands together. They sniff the *smoky smell*. It smells like winter!

Once they are cozy and warm, what could be better than drinking big, steaming mugs of *hot chocolate*? That makes them cozy and warm inside as well. And the rich chocolaty smell is almost as good as the taste!

"How about some *cookies* with our hot chocolate?" asks Mama, bringing in a tray.

"Oh boy!" say the cubs. "Cookies with hot chocolate! Perfect!"

"Yum! Cookies!" says Papa, grabbing a handful.
"Really, Papa!" scolds Mama, laughing. "Don't be greedy!"
"But," says Papa with his mouth full, "I'm a very big bear!"

Now that they're warm and well fed, the family can decorate their Christmas tree. They get out boxes of ornaments.

"We call these our *bearlooms*!" says Papa, hanging them carefully on the branches.

They add twinkly lights and finish up with red-striped candy canes.

"Smell that?" asks Mama, sniffing the candy canes. "That's *peppermint!*"

"Mmm!" they all sigh.

It's time to decorate the rest of the house. Mama and the cubs make fragrant creations by putting *cloves in oranges.* They set them around the house. They look very nice and have a strong, spicy smell. Their whole home is beginning to smell a lot like Christmas!

Now it's time to start cooking for Christmas dinner. Mama is the master chef, but Papa and the cubs all help out.
They start with a pan of *roasted chestnuts*. You need to cut an X in the shells before you cook them to let the steam escape.

Otherwise, the steam will make them pop! Papa does the cutting. There's nothing so Christmasy as the smell of chestnuts roasting on a fire!

One of Mama's specialties is old-fashioned *apple pie*. She sets the cubs to work peeling apples, and Papa slices them up. The juicy apples fill the kitchen with a delicious apple scent. It smells like an apple orchard in autumn.

One of the ingredients that makes apple pie so delicious is *ground cinnamon*. Mama adds the spicy brown powder. Honey gets a little up her nose. It makes her sneeze, AH-CHOO!

"Bless you!" they all laugh.

Bears love *honey*, and Mama
makes one of their favorite dishes—
honey nut cake. Mama pours the rich
golden honey into a mixing bowl
from the family honeypot. She lets
the cubs (and Papa) have a little taste.

The smell makes Papa think of his favorite bee tree.

The final touch is a batch of *gingerbread* bears.
They look just like Mama, Papa, and the cubs.

Papa bites the head right off his! Mama and
the cubs are shocked. But then they shrug and bite
the heads off theirs, too!

Have a yummy Christmas full of warm and
wonderful scents!